DATE DUE

MR 2 '93	JY 16 '09		
AP 14 '93			
AP 30 '93	NO 17 '11		
JE 15 '93			
SE 27 '93			
MAY 17 '95			
APR 07 '97			
AUG 08 '98			
AG 14 '99			
AG 20 '02			
9-30-03			

FILM FLUBS

Memorable Movie Mistakes

by Bill Givens

A Citadel Press Book
Published by Carol Publishing Group

Library of Congress Cataloging-in-Publication Data

Givens, Bill.
    Film flubs : memorable movie mistakes / by Bill Givens.
      p.   cm.
  "A Citadel Press book."
  ISBN 0-8065-1161-3 :
  1. Motion pictures--Humor. 2. Motion pictures--Miscellanea.
 I. Title.
 PN1994.9.G58   1990
 791.43--dc20   90-40481
                                                   CIP

10 9 8 7 6 5 4

ROSEBUD

(and we're not talking about a sled),

This One's For You

CONTENTS

ACKNOWLEDGMENTS

Many of the film flubs pointed out in this book come from the eyes of sharp-eyed, perspicacious film buffs—in which group, unfortunately, I cannot always count myself. I love to hear about the little errors that creep into films, but rarely can I spot them myself.

The inspiration for this book was an article I wrote for *Premiere* magazine, entitled "Movie Goofs," which detailed thirteen of the bloopers contained herein. My gratitude to editors Terri Minsky, Jill Kearney and Eliza Krause, and the magazine's staff researchers for their assistance with the article.

In accumulating the material used in this book, I owe a deep debt of gratitude to the staff of the Margaret Herrick Library at the Academy of Motion Picture Arts and Sciences in Los Angeles. It's always a pleasure to research film-related articles and books at the Herrick, and its staff is without peer in both filmic knowledge and helpfulness.

Many of the continuity errors contained herein have been listed in various publications, including *Premiere, Halliwell's Film Companion, USA Today,* and *Trivia Unlimited.* Wherever possible, the names of their contributors are included in the list of sharp-eyed and quick-witted gaffe spotters. Others have been pointed out in columns in the Hollywood trade papers, *Variety* and *The Hollywood Reporter,* in *The Los Angeles Times*' informative "Outtakes" column, and from innumerable magazine articles accumulated by the Motion Picture Academy's library.

I'm sure that some important names are inadvertently missed in the listing of contributors. All too often, on learning that I was writing this book, friends would tell me of their favorite film flubs...and unless I was alert enough to write them down at that moment (which isn't always the case), I may have added them to my list of flubs without making note of the source. Herewith, my apologies for any sins of omission.

My gratitude, also, for those who helped me—both physically and psychologically—bring this project to fruition; Bart Andrews, both an agent and himself an accomplished author; Craig Phillips; my dear friends Howard and Mary Lynn Gottfried, Liz and Nora; the guys at Video West, who not only helped me find tapes but also contributed some of their own favorite flubs; Leonard Maltin, for his valuable reference books, his help with magazine pieces, and his words of encouragement; Sue and Ray Ingle, Leroy Morganti, Effie Glassco; the kindly magazine editors who've kept me supplied with enough work to keep body and soul at the same address while I worked on *Film Flubs*; and my family for their encouragement and support.

Sources

"Masters in Blunderland," by Jean Fournier, Tower Video Collector, December 1989.

"Hi, Judy," by Robert Young, Jr., Tower Video Collector, September 1989.

"Untimely Mistakes," by John Horn, *American Film*, February 1990.

"Freeze Frame Movies," by David Hajdu, *Video Review*, October 1989.

"Big Screen Bloopers," by Bill Givens, *Premiere* magazine, October 1988.

Assorted articles, "Short Takes," edited by Terri Minsky, *Premiere* magazine, various issues.

"To Err Is, Er...Oz," by David Fradkin, *Los Angeles* magazine, March 1982.

"10 Greatest Movie Bloopers," *Star* magazine, April 1989.

"Movie Mistakes Hollywood Hoped You Wouldn't See," by Susan Fenton, *The National Enquirer*, July 1988.

"Blunders," by Heidi E. Capousis, *USA Today*, April 1988.

"Funny Flubs In Your Favorite Films," by Wendy McArdle, *The National Enquirer*, March 1989.

Assorted items in "Outtakes," various writers, *The Los Angeles Times*.

"Hollywood's Best Faux Pas," by Derrick Bang, *Pulse*, May 1986.

Hollywood Anecdotes, by Paul Boller and Ronald L. Davis, Ballantine Books 1987.

The Hollywood History of the World, by George MacDonald Fraser, Fawcett Columbine Books, 1988.

The Golden Turkey Awards, Harry and Michael Medved, Berkeley Books, 1981.

The Filmgoer's Companion, by Leslie Halliwell, Scribner's, 1988.

THE SHARP-EYED, QUICK-WITTED GAFFE SPOTTER SQUAD

Bart Andrews, Derrick Bang, Paul Boller, Gordon Bressack, Gary Butcher, Bradley G. Carr, Marc DeLeon, Paul Dini, Larry Ditellio, Buzz Dixon, Faith Ellen Dryer, Susan Fenton, Jean Fournier, Charles Goldstein, David Gonzales, David Hajdu, Ken Kahler, Tony Kalinski, Caroline Kirk, Jim Krueger, Alvin Marill, Jack Matthews, Wendy McArdle, Michael Medved, Janie Miller, Craig Modderno, Phillip David Morgan, Michael Muller, Phillip Railsback, Randy Rice, Mordecai Richler, Clark Risley, Hilary Roberts, David Robichaud, Merrill Shindler, Steve Tamerius, Tom Titus, Bill Warren, Dawn Watkins, Jeff Wheatcraft, Fred L. Worth, Mary Yronwode, Robert Young, Jr.

INTRODUCTION

The making of a movie is a complex and collaborative process. The work of a large number of people has to mesh to bring the film all the way from the initial concept to its fulfillment on the screen. Just take a look at all those names in a film's end credits. Every person had some important function in creating what you've just seen—and the credits don't always list *everybody* who was involved with the production. Along the way there's many an opportunity for little errors, slipups or missteps to creep into the process.

On the one hand, since so many people are working on the film, there are numerous opportunities to catch and correct errors of fact or logic, or technical gaffes. But, on the other, since the talents of so many people can be involved in a typical movie, there's plenty of opportunity for things to happen that don't get caught—until they're spotted on the screen by a really sharp-eyed viewer.

In Hollywood lingo, film gaffes, goofs and slipups are known as "continuity errors." Most of the time, they're the result of interruptions in the continuity of the script—the logical flow of the story and the pictures from beginning to end. By definition, "continuity" is the orderly progression of the film's action from shot to shot for the proper development of the story.

By and large, the job of maintaining continuity falls to the script supervisor. If you've ever been on a movie set—or seen pictures of one—it's easy to spot the script supervisor. That's the person who has a large notebook permanently in hand and a stopwatch around the neck, and who will usually be working only a few footsteps away from the director.

The script supervisor must have the eyes of an eagle and a court reporter's ability to note the most minute details. The job requires keeping up with everything on the set—from the visual, such as the location of every piece of furniture and prop and every change of costume on each actor, to the logical continuity of the action that happened in the scene before and what will happen in the scene coming up next. Never mind that movies are rarely shot in page-to-page sequence. All of these details have to be kept in mind, whether or not the scene was shot yesterday or last week, or won't even be shot for another week or so.

Stuart Lippman, a former president of the script supervisor's union, says that the job of its members is to watch everything from the part in an actor's hair to the length of a partially-smoked cigarette. Since scenes are often shot hours or days apart, a "mismatch" from one scene to another can cause a distracting, even embarrassing, jump in the film.

"Even with weeks and weeks of post-production, some things seem to slip through," Lippman says. "By and large, we catch most of them on the set—but after that, it's pretty much out of our hands. It's really up to each craft—cameramen, wardrobe, whatever—to make sure that there are no goofs in their aspect of the production."

The script supervisor's responsibility originally fell to the producer's secretary, but as it evolved into a separate job, the secretaries became "script girls," then script clerks, and now script (or continuity) supervisors. Even though for many years the profession was made up almost entirely of women, many men are script supervisors these days. He or she gets involved with the film a few weeks before production begins. Notes are made for each scene, then the script supervisor is on the set from before the time the cameras roll each day until the last shot is made—usually around twelve to fifteen hours. The supervisor watches and records every aspect of each day's work, feeds lines to actors when necessary, and works hand-in-hand with the director to keep the filming process flowing. Even in post-production, the script supervisor often helps the director and film editor find just the right take for a particular scene or dialogue nuance, even if the film hasn't been developed.

＊ ＊ ＊

Meanwhile, back on the set, think of the complexity of shooting a scene as simple as the act of entering a hotel room from a hallway. In the first place the hallway (or a set representing the hallway) has to be dressed with props, lights set up and aimed, camera angles established, the actors' movements worked out, dialogue rehearsed. Ultimately the scene is shot. Several takes may be required for any number of reasons—a line flub, a blown light, an extraneous noise, or perhaps just for the director or actor's peace of mind.

13

Then the scene is "wrapped," the actors go back to their trailers, and the cameras and lights are moved to the other side of the door. The process starts all over again, and since several hours can pass between the shooting of the views from outside of the door and those from the inside of the room, there's plenty of opportunity for a slipup. The actors might take off their costumes—especially if they're going to eat lunch, take a nap, or study their lines—and once they've re-dressed, everything has to be the same and in the same place, from jewelry to neckties.

By the time the cameras, lights and various other accoutrements of the process are reset, there's many an opportunity for some minor glitch to occur.

Even a conversation between two characters can be extremely involved. First the scene is shot from one actor's point of view, with the camera looking over the shoulder of the person being spoken to. Then the camera is moved to shoot the "reverses," looking from the other actor's point of view. Again, time passes as the equipment is moved, cameras refocused, lights repositioned, backgrounds moved into place, and extras blocked in for "atmosphere." Watch as actor A talks to actor B in a film. First, you'll see the camera shooting over B's shoulder toward A. Throughout the scene you'll see shots cut back and forth between the two actors—filmed over each other's shoulder. The cameras usually aren't moved for each alternating line. First, all of actor A's lines are shot over B's shoulder, then A repeats his lines as they are shot from B's point of view, and B does his lines from A's point of view. The back-and-forth cuts that make the conversation work come in the editing room.

A day's work on a film set can range from the shooting of one page of the script—less than a minute—to about three pages on a really good, fast-moving work day. Since the average film script is around 110 pages, time before the cameras can range from weeks to months.

This process of putting a movie together bit by bit means that every little detail has to be watched and duplicated from one shot to the next.

The set itself and the props that are used to "dress" it open up a world of opportunities for continuity slips. Sets are usually roped off and marked with "hot set" banners to keep casual visitors or cleanup crews from moving anything from one day to the next. But, things happen, and somehow the little gremlins slip in and move a vase from one table to another...turn a sculpture in a different direction...cause a picture to slant. And if the goof makes it to the finished film, someone out there inevitably will spot it.

Flowers are a particular problem, and more often than not, realistic "fakes" are used—since a real flower that wilted overnight would cause a distracting "jump" in the picture. But even the ordinary props used in a film can cause problems. Take cigarettes, for instance—in more than one film, a cigarette has gone from long to short to long again during a scene. Keeping the liquid at the right level in beverages can drive the prop people mad, too. Watch Jane Fonda's *The Morning After* (1986) and notice how the level of the wine in a bottle rises and falls in a single "continuous" scene.

Anachronisms are another nagging continuity error, popping up when references to events that haven't happened yet show up in an actor's dialogue—or when props or costume accessories are used before their time (wristwatches are among the major offenders).

Then there are errors of fact or logic. Film scripts are usually gone over carefully for accuracy, both by the writers and by researchers who specialize in the field. But, nobody's perfect.

Joan Pearce, who works with Kellum DeForest, one of the film industry's leading researchers, says that even though scripts are carefully examined for factual errors, anachronisms, problematic character names, or anything for which the studio could be sued, script researchers generally don't get the chance to see the "dailies," so what happens between script approval and the actual shooting is out of their hands.

There are even some gaffes which, while appearing to be errors, really aren't. These are the ones done deliberately for some reason, usually an artistic effect. A shot from Garbo's classic *Queen Christina* (1933) has been cited as such an example. On looking at the film's dramatic closing scene as she sails off into exile, you'll notice that the breeze which blows Garbo's hair comes from a different direction than the wind which fills the sails directly behind her. Could it be that the director set it up that way to make the shot more glamorous and effective? And there have been instances where flags and banners flew contrary to wind direction—in order to make the overall effect look good on the screen.

Given the number of opportunities for slipups, it's amazing that so few actually make it into the movies. But they do, and many a film buff delights in being the first to spot a continuity error on screen.

Remember, too, that gaffes aren't the exclusive province of the low-budget or casual filmmakers. In this book, you'll find continuity errors which appear in some of the all-time great films, classics such as *Gone With the Wind*, *The Ten Commandments* and *North By Northwest*, as well as modern-day hits *The Shining*, *Jagged Edge*, *Who Framed Roger Rabbit* and *Raiders of the Lost Ark*, not to mention movies ranging right down to Grade Z goodies and drive-in specials.

Then there's an entire category of films in which the errors are so obvious or so plentiful that they deserve a book unto themselves—memorable movies like *Plan 9 From Outer Space* (1959), the classic which "Golden Turkey" mavens Harry and Michael Medved judge "stands the test of time to emerge as *the* bad film of all time." Or 1963's never-to-be-forgotten *They Saved Hitler's Brain* (aka *Madmen of Mandoras*), in which the entire cast changes mid-film.

Most of the films mentioned in this book are available on home video. Be aware that it's often difficult to spot a gaffe on video—due to the fact that the screen is so small that the picture resolution is not nearly so sharp as it is on a forty-foot one in a theater, and that when you watch a televised movie, more often than not it's been "panned and scanned." On TV, you're seeing only about two-thirds of the picture, to accommodate it to the squarish dimensions of the television screen, which is quite a different ratio from the more or less rectangular film screen. The portion of the picture that you see in the "pan and scan" version is chosen at the discretion of the copying editor, since it's practically impossible to get the entire picture on a television screen, unless it's done in the "letterbox" method with a black band at the bottom and top of the screen. (And the "pan and scan" can lead to its own category of continuity problems, such as the video of a Fred Astaire picture in which his partner dances off the screen and back on again.)

Although home video has revolutionized the film business, the only real way to see a movie remains on the big screen at a motion picture theater. And if you want to experience a movie in the fullest of its cinematic possibilities, avoid the mall multiplexes and see it at a single-screen theater, preferably by beating the bulldozers to one of the great movie palaces.

This book contains gaffes from more than 180 films. But the work of Hollywood's cinema industry over the years encompasses literally thousands of films, most of which have escaped unscathed by discernable errors—or perhaps their mistakes haven't been caught yet!

At any rate, there's no entertainment quite like a movie, and this book is dedicated to all the craftsmen and women who work to bring this particular art form to entertain, inform, even frighten you. Go to a movie. Enjoy. And...when you spot a gaffe, let us know!

MOVING IMAGES

Little gaffes and slipups often can be caused by the inattention that comes from time delays—the hours or days that can elapse between shots.

Take, for example, Jane Fonda and Robert Redford's stroll during *Barefoot in the Park* (1967). As the pair walks away from the camera, Fonda is on Redford's right. In the very next shot, a reversal where they continue the stroll, this time facing the camera, Fonda has slipped over to his left side.

Other examples of when left isn't right and right is wrong:

SAY IT ISN'T SO, RAY

Field of Dreams was one of the sleeper hits of 1989—but someone was sleeping on the mound when they let Ray Liotta, playing Shoeless Joe Jackson, bat right-handed. The real Shoeless Joe was a southpaw.

21

Perhaps the filmmakers should have taken a cue from veteran director Sam Wood, who had a similar problem when he worked with Gary Cooper in *Pride of the Yankees* (1942). Cooper, too, was right-handed, and he was playing Lou Gehrig, one of baseball's most famous left-handed batters. Try as he might, Cooper could not bat left-handed. Editor Danny Mandell suggested having Cooper bat right-handed, then run to third base instead of first. Mandell merely flipped the film over in the editing room, and all was well. Of course, to make the effect work, the costumer had to sew reversed numbers on the uniforms of all the players who appeared in the shot!

BRUSH IT AGAIN, SAM

Humphrey Bogart is brushing his hair in *The Roaring Twenties* (1939) with the brush in his right hand, as he talks to James Cagney. In the very next shot, though, the brush is in Bogie's left hand.

CHANGING PLACES

Look for a bottle of beer to move from the towel dispenser on the left to the one on the right during a restroom visit from "brothers" Danny De-Vito and Arnold Schwarzenegger in *Twins* (1988).

THEY WENT THATAWAY

By most standards, *Lawrence of Arabia* (1962) is one of the greatest films ever made. But even T. E. Lawrence's desert epic isn't without a flaw. Guess who our fearless flaw-spotter is, in this instance? None other than the director himself, David Lean. Lean told an interviewer that when he was reconstructing the film for its 1989 re-release, he noticed that in one scene, camels went from left to right in the first reel, then right to left in the second. Then he noticed that Peter O'Toole's wristwatch was on the wrong arm in the second reel. "It turns out that they'd flopped an entire reel," Lean told an interviewer. "They'd flopped the whole damn thing."

The error apparently happened when the 35mm print was struck in 1966. All of the theatrical, video and TV prints of *Lawrence of Arabia* since that time contain ten minutes of film with reversed images—a gaffe that has now been corrected.

SOMEBODY TOUCHED IT

A dead body moves from one part of the room to another in *The Untouchables* (1987), even though nobody touches it.

HELP ME COLLAR THE CROOKS

And while we're on the subject of *The Untouchables*...when Kevin Costner visits Sean Connery's apartment to ask for his Scottish-burred mentor's help, pay close attention to Connery's carefully-buttoned collar. During one cut, he turns to face Costner. As he starts to turn, the collar is buttoned, but when he spins all the way around, the collar is casually open.

CASTING DOUBT

In Alfred Hitchcock's 1954 classic *Rear Window*, wheelchair-bound James Stewart, his left leg in a cast, spends his time spying on his neighbors through binoculars. He must have had some problems with his right leg, too. If you watch very closely during a scene where he argues with Grace Kelly, you'll see a brief moment when the cast switches from the left leg to the right!

WHEELIES

Sean Connery and Jill St. John elude pursuers by tipping a Mustang onto
its right wheels and driving sideways through a narrow alley in *Diamonds
Are Forever* (1971). The Mustang emerges from the alley on its two left
wheels. (Since the Bond films are often replete with inside jokes, there's
some speculation that the narrow alley sequence was an intentional continuity error.)

WHEN THINGS GET HAIRY

Actors, being human (well, most of them), grow hair—or, in some cases, lose it. And when the filming of a movie stretches over weeks and months, stylists have to play close attention to hair length, lest it get away from them and cause a bit of cinematic weirdness. (Generally a film would be shot in reverse sequence so that an actor with long hair or a beard could have it shortened rather than having to wait until it grows.)

CLOSE SHAVE

John Wayne looks like a spry young whippersnapper brandishing a cavalry sword as he leads his troops into battle in the ads for John Ford's *Rio Grande* in 1950. The Duke's clean shaven, whether thwarting Apache uprisings or elsewhere romancing Maureen O'Hara. In the film itself, however, he's kind of world-weary and throughout sports a bushy mustache and a small goatee. Same can be said of his earlier *She Wore a Yellow Ribbon*—but scratch the goatee.

DUKING IT OUT

In his classic *North to Alaska* (1960), John Wayne loses his hairpiece during a fight scene...but in the next shot, the rug's right back on again.

31

It happened in *The Wizard of Oz* (1939). Judy Garland's hair changes length at least three times during the course of the film. When Dorothy is brought to the Wicked Witch's castle, her hair is mid-length. When Toto runs away, the tresses are down to her belt; and when the witch turns the hourglass, Dorothy's hair is up to her shoulders.

10/31/38
Original Dress
own Hair & fall
before darkening

THE WET LOOK

Mandy Patinkin's wet hair changes shape from shot to shot in a scene from *The Princess Bride* (1987).

But an even more unusual occurrence came in Roger Corman's quickie *The Terror* (1963), a film shot in a haphazard manner in order to get some extra life from the sets of *The Raven* (1963). Boris Karloff's scenes were done over a period of three days, while the sets were being torn down around him. Lines were delivered at random, before the script was written. But Jack Nicholson's scenes were shot on weekends over a period of months—allowing you to see his hairline recede during the course of the film.

LOST HORIZONS

Since so many films are made in Los Angeles, it's common for residents to spot little continuity slips involving the local landscape. By and large, they won't be noticed by anyone who lives outside the city, and frequently they're necessary to avoid traffic problems or to make the setting conform to the script.

Example: In 1989's *Lethal Weapon II*, a chase scene begins when Mel Gibson backs out of a driveway on Mulholland Drive. But when he switches gear from reverse to forward, he's heading down the Angeles Crest Highway, miles away across the San Fernando Valley. Mulholland Drive is a busy mountaintop thoroughfare lined with some of the most expensive homes in Los Angeles. The odds against being able to film a successful chase scene on Mulholland are fairly high, even though it has been done in several movies. But the rugged, twistier highway through the Angeles National Forest makes for much more exciting chases.

And who but a Londoner would be alert to the fact that in *Knock on Wood* (1954) Danny Kaye turns a corner on Oxford Street and is instantly three miles away on Ludgate Hill? Or that Van Johnson's Portman Square apartment in *23 Paces to Baker Street* (1956) has a river view which rightfully belongs two miles away at the Savoy Hotel? Now you know.

So, speaking of fractured geography, you might as well know that...

COAST-TO-COAST VISION

Watch the camera shift as Kevin Bacon (in the 1985 *Quicksilver*) bicycles down a New York street, to his point of view, and marvel with him as his eyes suddenly behold a street in San Francisco, without ever stopping for a red light. In fact, cross-country vision aside, you'll even notice a bus cross Bacon's path bearing on it side an advertisement for a West Coast radio station.

SO WHAT DOES A VAMPIRE KNOW FROM GEOGRAPHY?

Bela Lugosi refers to the town of Whitby as "so close to London" in the 1931 *Dracula*. Whitby is 254 miles away.

CROSS COUNTRY FLYING

In *Big Business* (1988), the airport that is supposedly New York's JFK is actually Los Angeles' LAX.

WHERE EAST MEETS WEST

The 1969 volcano epic is entitled *Krakatoa, East of Java*. Ahem. Beg pardon. The island of Krakatoa is actually *west* of Java...a problem obviously sidestepped when the videocassette release was retitled *Volcano*.

EASTWARD, INTO THE SETTING SUN

It's a very dramatic ending...in *The Green Berets* (1968), John Wayne walks down the beach, his arm around the young Vietnamese boy, as the sun sets on the ocean behind him. Beg pardon, Mr. Wayne, sir. Perhaps you didn't realize that the beaches in Vietnam face east?

EASTWARD, INTO THE SETTING SUN II (The Sequel)

The closing shot of the 1988 *Sunset* carries the supertitle: "And that's the way it really happened...Give or take a lie or two." But...in the drama of the moment, as Bruce Willis waves goodbye to James Garner, did they notice that one of the lies was that the train bearing Garner back east from Pasadena, California, was heading toward a glorious sunset over the San Gabriel Mountains, which are, of course, east of Pasadena? And so, as the sun sets in the East...

...and that's the way it really happened. Give or take a lie or two.

39

GONNA' BUILD ME A MOUNTAIN

In William Faulkner's novel as well as the movie of *The Reivers* (1969), the setting is in Northern Mississippi and in Memphis, both located in an area that's pretty flat, except for some low, rolling hills with no sign of a mountain anywhere on the horizon. But the horse race scene has as its backdrop a range of towering, rugged mountains. It was shot in California.

There's an inside joke in the film, too. William Faulkner, on whose story the film is based, named the whorehouse "Binford's" after Memphis' notorious movie censor, Lloyd T. Binford.

THE EDITOR GOOFED

The film may be in the can…but it often takes a brilliant editor to keep the entire movie out of the can. The work of this craftsman can be the difference between a great movie and a mediocre one.

Movies, as we all know, are shot in many short segments, called "takes," and the director and editor have to choose which ones show off the best performance or do the best job of moving the story along.

It's up to the editor to make sure the film flows seamlessly, and at the same time assemble it in such a fashion that it's visually interesting and involving, all the while taking the story to its conclusion. And a good editor can often find just the right shot or sequence to cover a director, cameraman, or actor's mistakes.

But what editor among us is perfect? A few cases in point:

HAS ANYBODY SEEN OLD WHATSHISNAME?

Steve McQueen stars as a bounty hunter in *Tom Horn* (1980). But perhaps there should have been a bounty on the head of the editor who spliced in one scene so that an actor got up from a table and instantly disappeared!

BACKWARDS THINKING

Early in *Robocop* (1987), we see cars racing toward Dallas' famed Reunion Tower, the great golf ball in the sky. But when the shot changes to a reverse angle, the cars are speeding *away* from the tower, even though they have not changed direction. Something went wrong somewhere!

BACKWARDS THINKING II (The Sequel)

Similar to the *Robocop* slipup, is the one when in *Carrie* (1976), director Brian de Palma had Sissy Spacek walk slowly backwards from a car in order to create the dream sequence car crash. Then the film was speeded up and run backwards to make it appear that the car was hitting Carrie. But another car accidentally got in the shot, and you can see it flash by, driving in reverse.

NOT THE GREATEST EDIT ON EARTH

Several early shots in De Mille's *The Greatest Show on Earth* (1952) use the same background, edited in with the blue-screen matte process. When the editor cuts from shot to shot, the actors appear to be zapping back and forth, since there's no change in the size of the background.

THE OTHER SIDE OF THE WINDOW

When a movie is being shot on a soundstage, set designers sometime
project background scenes onto the window frames to create the illusion
of a real window. However, in *The Other Side of Midnight* (1977), someone
goofed and switched the projection plates from one scene to another.
First, you see mountains from a bedroom window. Then, in the next
scene, you see the ocean in the very same window.

WELL, THEN, JUST SHOOT IT DOWN

In the 1964 *Fail-Safe*, a pilot, chasing a runaway B-52 bomber, is told to use his afterburners to increase his speed. As soon as we see him engage the afterburners in the cockpit, there is a cut and we see the aircraft launch its rockets, instead. Wrong footage.

45

MIS-M*A*S*H

Boston film reviewer Nat Segaloff reports a series of confusing edits in Robert Altman's classic *M*A*S*H* (1970). First, there's the subplot about Ho-John, the mess-hall attendant who is filled with amphetamines by the 4077th medics to attempt to keep him out of the Korean military. He is dropped off at the examination center, and that's the (supposed) end of the sub-plot. Later, however Ho-John turns up as a war casualty in a brief scene. He's the "body" for which the doctors get blood by tapping into a sleeping Colonel Blake. Ho-John is lying on his side on the operating table before expiring and it's his body covered with a sheet atop a jeep behind where a poker game is later being played. The game is somber, and the camera arcs around it as the doctors stare out of the tent at the jeep. This, Segaloff says, explains the focus on the corpse in a film strewn with them. Ho-John is not just one more corpse, and footage explaining how he became a war casualty must be somewhere on the cutting room floor.

Another sequence shift comes when Major "Hot Lips" Houlihan (Sally Kellerman) arrives at the 4077th. Altman brought her in earlier and made her a major character in the film. But, if you look closely, when she gets off the helicopter, you can see Lt. "Dish" (Jo Ann Pflug) already in it. She is leaving as Hot Lips is arriving, although, since the continuity has been shifted around in the editing room, she has scenes still to come.

And...Segaloff alerts viewers to look at a scene showing the feet of the surgeons early in the operating room sequences. You can hear Elliott Gould's voice, even though his character is not introduced for another ten minutes.

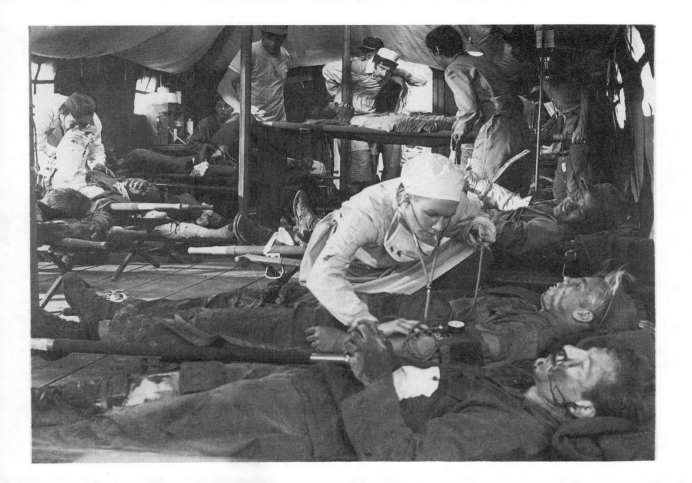

COSTUME CHANGES

At London's Elstree Studios, prim Elaine Scheyreck faced quite a dilemma. As a costumer, she spent plenty of time in the company of actors who were stripped down to their bare essentials—still, she was faced with something she preferred not to discuss. Just back from viewing the dailies of *Superman*, Ms. Scheyreck now had to tell the producers that a scene had to be re-shot because Christopher Reeve's "private parts" jumped from one side to the other in his tight-fitting costume.

Had the error not been caught and corrected, somewhere along the way audiences would have had a real laugh—probably at a most inappropriate time—when Reeve's goodies flew from one side to the other in mid-scene.

From that day forward, one of Elaine Scheyreck's duties was to make sure that the handsome actor's pants bulge was in the right place every day—and since multiple costume changes were required because Reeve would get sweaty during the complex flying scenes, it was finally decided to eliminate the problem completely by having a "swim cup" sewn into the Superman outfits.

STANDING IN THE SHADES

While standing in the doorway talking to Spencer Tracy in *Broken Lance* (1954), Katy Jurado is wearing a dress that changes color in alternate shots as she converses.

SARONG COLLECTION

Loni Anderson finds herself marooned on a desert island with Perry King and a teeny-weeny overnight case in the TV movie *Stranded* (1986), but the teeny-weeny case manages to provide her with not only enough shades of blush for a year's worth of intimate candlelight rendezvous but also an amazing assortment of revealing sarongs. (And she was only on a quick business trip.)

ANATOMY OF AN ERROR

There's a curious problem in Otto Preminger's 1959 *Anatomy of a Murder*. Oddly enough, Lana Turner had walked off the picture, and Preminger said that it was because she didn't like her costumes. Turner replied, "I would not walk out of a picture for anything as trivial as a costume." But Preminger, vowing to take a lesser "star" and make her "a new Lana Turner," cast Lee Remick in the role. The controversy must have broken the concentration of the costumers. Watch Remick as she prepares to leave the cafe in a pivotal scene. She sashays to the door wearing a lovely, flowing skirt, but coming out the door to the street, she has on tight-fitting slacks!

NUMBERS GAME

In *Jailhouse Rock* (1957), Elvis Presley is seen at one point wearing uniform #6239; in another scene, his number magically becomes #6240. Was he promoted for good behavior or great rock 'n' rollin'?

The studio retouched this '41 publicity still for *Reap the Wild Wind*

...Just check the dude with the shades in the original.

Movies are shot in bits and pieces, and maintaining costume continuity from shot to shot can be quite a challenge. The average "take" covers only a few seconds of the action, and an entire day's work may move the story along only a couple of minutes. The scene which is started today may be finished tomorrow, the next day, or even months later. To take advantage of set and location economies, scenes are often shot out of context—the end may well be filmed long before the beginning—and therein lies the opportunity for many a goof to slip into the footage.

We're not just talking low-budget specials, either. Costume glitches have crept into the classics, and they continue to pop up in many of today's big-budget blockbusters.

CHANGING OF THE COLORS

In *North By Northwest* (1959), the only suit that Cary Grant carries with him is light blue-gray, when he's in the Chicago hotel; dark gray out on the prairie. Hitchcock said it wasn't an error—he blamed it on the lighting.

IF THE SHOE FITS

As Kathleen Turner jumps from a rooftop onto a train in *The Jewel of the Nile* (1985), she's wearing canvas slip-ons. But then she slips and falls—and as she clings to the side of the rail car, notice that she's wearing leather sandals. Then, following her rescue, she's back in the canvas shoes again.

SWIRLING SKIRTS

In *Silk Stockings*, the 1957 musical remake of the classic *Ninotchka*, comely Russian Commissar Cyd Charisse wears a flowing gray skirt with a front seam sewn all the way to the hem. As she swirls and twirls with Fred Astaire, her attire changes from skirt to culottes and back again. In several of the dance turns, it's very obvious that she's wearing a skirt. In the scenes where she does splits and larger steps, the outfit is split into more modest culottes.

DISORDER IN THE COURT

When Glenn Close and Jeff Bridges enter the courtroom in *Jagged Edge* (1985), she is wearing a gray suit. Then she makes her opening arguments standing before the judge wearing a dark blue suit and a white blouse. A few minutes later (without having time to go home and change), she questions a witness while wearing a dark brown suit and a light brown blouse.

CATHY AND HEATHCLIFFE WENT UP THE HILL...

Heading up the hill to meet Heathcliffe in *Wuthering Heights* (1939), Merle Oberon's Cathy drapes a shawl over her shoulders. She is wearing a blouse and a full-length skirt. Somewhere between the bottom of the hill and the top, she must have found a dressing room and changed clothes—or stopped off and left the clothes she was wearing at the Moor-side cleaners. When she reaches the top where her brooding lover waits, she's wearing an entirely different, tailored dress and no shawl.

DELIVER US FROM...

In Martin Scorsese's *The Last Temptation of Christ* (1988), Willem Dafoe as Jesus not only wears a robe that has double-seamed machine sewing, but when he turns around you can see the stitching where a label is sewn in (are we talking Armani, here?). Similarly, in Disney's 1952 *The Story of Robin Hood*, Joan Rice's Maid Marian wears a dress with a clearly visible zipper. It happened again in *Jason and the Argonauts* (1963), when one of the dancing priestesses has a zipper in her costume.

HOW'S THAT AGAIN, SAM?

After more than forty-six years of being one of history's most-watched movies, no one seemed to notice that the wardrobe department blew it when they dressed Ingrid Bergman for a flashback scene in *Casablanca* (1942). Bergman's Ilsa remembers wearing a dress when she and Bogart's Rick parted months before in Paris. But when Ted Turner's perspicacious colorizers got a closer look at the film, they discovered that Ilsa was actually wearing a suit.

"I never noticed that, and I've seen that film many times," Turner Entertainment President Roger Mayer, who supervised the colorization process, told the *Los Angeles Times*. "I don't think many people would." But somebody did.

IN THE TIME TUNNEL

Anachronisms—the little slips that show an actor wearing a prop that wasn't invented at the time of a movie, singing a song that hadn't been written yet, or even using language that wasn't appropriate to the period—can move a film out of reality into its very own time tunnel.

Anachronisms go all the way back to Shakespeare (and even further, I'm sure). Old Willie slipped up when he had a character refer to a clock in *Julius Caesar*, since the best they could do at the time (around 100 B.C.) was use a sundial. (Couldn't you just imagine Sylvester Stallone doing the part—"Yo, Hadrian!")

A good anachronism always delights the serious gaffe-meister. One of the jobs of the script researchers is to check diligently to ensure that these things don't happen. But they can goof. Even more probable is that an actor ad-libs a line long after the script is out of the hands of the researchers, at which point there's nothing that they can do about it.

Consider also *Mutiny on the Bounty* which, although filmed in 1935, was set in the 1700s. Charles Laughton, as Captain Bligh, uses the word "sabotage"—a word that did not enter the language until the 20th century, circa World War I.

In an article in *American Film*, John Horn points out several instances of what he calls "anti-semanticisms," such as characters in Eddie Murphy's *Harlem Nights* (1989), set in the Depression era, using such modern expressions as "I'll let you have your space," "Can we get back to you," "Yo," and "I just need a couple of seconds to get my head together."

And he points out that in the 1940s-era *In the Mood*, the 1980s term "Life's a bitch and then you die" slips into Phil Alden Robinson's carefully-researched dialogue.

Similarly, in *The Scalphunters* (1968), Ossie Davis mentions the planet Pluto. The film takes place in the 1800s. Pluto, the outermost planet in our solar system, was not discovered until the 1930s.

Speaking of centuries, in *Kings Row* (1942), Ann Sheridan, playing Randy Monoghan, wrote "Happy New Year" in the snow. Ronald Reagan (remember him?), as her beau Drake McHugh, scratched it out and wrote "Century." The date was January 1, 1900. Don't tell Ronnie, but the 20th century didn't begin until January 1, 1901.

Catching anachronisms and historical errors in movies requires a sharp eye and a discerning mind. Many screen goofs pass by so quickly that most of us don't even notice...or, if we do, they just don't register. But if there's a slipup, there's sure to be someone out there who will spot it. Cases in point:

WHO FRAMED THE PASADENA FREEWAY?

In *Who Framed Roger Rabbit* (1988), there is much conversation about the plot to tear down "Toontown" to build the world's first freeway—from Hollywood to Pasadena, California. *Roger Rabbit* is set in 1947. However, the Pasadena freeway was already in place, having been built in 1940.

BRIDGE TO NOWHERE

While we're tooling around London, it should be pointed out that in *The Lodger* (1944), the Tower Bridge is shown, even though the film is set ten years before the famed span was built.

ET WHAT, ELIZABETH?

It's one of the most majestic scenes in all filmdom, when Elizabeth Taylor, that noted Egyptian, enters Rome in a regal procession in the 1963 *Cleopatra*. On her way into town, she passes under a triumphal arch—one that wasn't built until after the real Cleo's death in 30 B.C.

A CRATE WITH NO STATE

The Sound of Music (1965) was also set in the 1930s. In the scene where Julie Andrews takes the children to the market, several gaffe-spotters have pointed out that there is a crate stamped "Jaffa Oranges—Product of Israel." The State of Israel was not founded until May 1948. However, the "pan and scan" appears to have eliminated this gaffe from the video version of the film when it moves in on a dropped tomato.

WE ARE SIAMESE, IF YOU PLEASE

So goes the lyric from *Lady and the Tramp*. But someone should have told the Spielberg/Lucas crowd that in 1936, the time in which their movie, *Raiders of the Lost Ark* (1981) was set, the country that we call Thailand was still Siam. Early in *Raiders*, Indy's route is traced by a small airplane flying over a map which identifies one of the countries as Thailand. Sorry, guys, Siam did not become Thailand until 1939.

BEFORE TIME BEGAN

In *Emma Hamilton* (1969), England's audible landmark, Big Ben, is heard striking in the background. Normally, this wouldn't be unusual—except that the historical romance takes place in 1804, a mere 50 years before Big Ben was built.

CRUISIN' INTO THE FUTURE

Just as the title tells us, the movie *Cruisin '57* is set in 1957. So why is one character wearing an "Evel Knievel" T-shirt...since the canyon-jumping daredevil was a '70s phenomenon?

I DUB THEE SIR JOHNSON & SIR JOHNSON

Medieval King Arthur (Richard Harris), while expounding on the joys of his mythical kingdom, wears a band-aid on the back of his neck in *Camelot* (1967).

NICE TO MEET YOU, SIR

Lionel Jeffries' character first meets King Arthur about an hour into *Camelot* (1967). But twenty minutes earlier, he is clearly visible at the King's wedding.

AERIAL ERRORS

Mysterious Island, made in 1961, is set a hundred years earlier, in 1860. But when a hot air balloon rises into the sky, it emerges from a nest of television antennas.

And in *The Wrong Box* (1966), a similar problem arises—TV antennas are seen on the roofs of homes in England's Victorian era.

TIRE TREADS IN THE SANDS OF TIME

The narrow wheels of the coach in John Ford's 1939 classic *Stagecoach* travel through wide tracks made by modern tires as they did in countless (mostly lower-budgeted) Westerns.

STARS AND STRIPES FOREVER

Throughout cinematic history, filmmakers have had problems in getting the proper American flag in their shots. Sometimes the prop person merely grabs the nearest flag, and doesn't count the stars. Other times, the current version of Old Glory may be flying on a nearby building. For example, there's such a scene in *The Godfather* (1972). It takes place in 1945, and you can see a 50-star flag. In 1945 there were only 48 states.

FLAGS FROM HEAVEN

A similar problem cropped up in the 1981 *Pennies From Heaven*. Bernadette Peters as Eileen Everson holds forth in a classroom which has a chart of flags on the wall. The film takes place in 1934, and many of the flags did not come into existence until years later, including those of Canada and Barbados.

BEFORE BREAKFAST?

Staying on the subject of *Pennies From Heaven*, one sharp-eyed viewer noticed that in the background is a 1934 billboard from Carole Lombard's *Love Before Breakfast*—a film which was made in 1936.

And while we're at it, it should be pointed out that *Annie* (1982) took place in 1933. At one point in the film, Daddy Warbucks takes Orphan Annie to see Garbo's *Camille* at Radio City Music Hall which he has "bought out" for the afternoon. Interesting, since the Garbo classic wasn't made until 1936—and it played not at Radio City Music Hall (which at the time showed primarily RKO and Columbia movies), but at the Capitol Theatre on Broadway, MGM's showcase in New York.

BYE, BYE, THE FOURTH OF JULY

Things looked pretty authentic when *Born on the Fourth of July* (1989) covered the 1968-69 era...but the song played in the background was Don McLean's "American Pie," which wasn't released until 1971.

Shall we continue? Here's an interesting situation—a "time tunnel" continuity gaffe in a film about time travel! At Mackinaw Island's Grand Hotel on June 27, 1912, in *Somewhere in Time* (1980), a guest hums and sings "You Made Me Love You." The song was copyrighted in 1913, the year that Al Jolson sang it in *The Honeymoon Express*.

And there's more. *Grease II* (1982) takes place in 1961. At the bowling alley, you can hear "Our Day Will Come" by Ruby and the Romantics playing in the background. The Ruby and the Romantics recording wasn't released until 1963.

LOST ON THE HORIZON

Both Mary McCarthy's book *The Group* and the movie made from it in 1966 are set in the Thirties. However, on the Manhattan skyline in several scenes of the film you can see the distinctive Pan Am Building, built in the Sixties.

THE TIME OF MUSIC

Getting music into its proper era can be a bedeviling problem—one that wasn't overcome in the 1953 movie *The Eddie Cantor Story*. It's 1904, and Cantor sings "Meet Me Tonight in Dreamland"—a song that was written in 1909.

It happened again in *Thoroughly Modern Millie* (1967), wherein one of the big production numbers is "Baby Face." *Millie* was set in 1922, four years before that song was written.

And in one of the two television movies in 1988 about Liberace, a flashback sequence had Lee playing piano in a 1934 Milwaukee dive while the chanteuse sang "The Man That Got Away"—which wasn't to be written for another 20 years!

TILL THE SONGS ROLL OUT

Till the Clouds Roll By, the lavish 1946 MGM musical that purported to be the life of Jerome Kern, in one sequence has Robert Walker (as Kern), a copy of Edna Ferber's *Show Boat* under his arm after being urged by songwriting pal Oscar Hammerstein II to read it as a possible next project, stopping by to see a supperclub act of a friend's daughter. Lucille Bremer is the performer and she announces to the audience that she'll next do a song that's been sweeping the country, Jerome Kern's "I Won't Dance" (with a zoot-suited Van Johnson). The time has to be around 1926 as Kern had yet to have a go at *Show Boat*, but "I Won't Dance" wasn't introduced to the public until his show *Roberta* premiered in 1933.

VAMPIN' AND TRAMPIN'

In the 1979 television movie, *The Triangle Factory Fire Scandal*, the girls in the sweatshop, to break the tension during a rest period on the eve of the conflagration, decide to entertain one another by doing Charlie Chaplin imitations and dressing up as his famous "Little Tramp." The fire—and the setting of the movie—was in 1911. Chaplin was virtually unknown in this country until 1914.

HEAVEN COULDN'T WAIT

The British *Quadrophenia*, which marked Sting's acting debut, was filmed in 1979 with the action taking place in 1964. Look for the movie house playing Warren Beatty's *Heaven Can Wait*, which was released in 1978.

DISPLACED SUBURBS

Although *The 'Burbs* (1989) is set in middle America, in some of the shots one can see The Disney Channel's office building in the background. It was filmed on the back lot of Universal Studios, just across the San Fernando Valley from the Disney Channel's headquarters in Burbank, California.

INTOLERABLE

In one of the greatest scenes of one of the greatest films of all time, one of D. W. Griffith's assistants is seen in a coat and tie as the Persians storm a wall in ancient Babylon in *Intolerance* (1916).

FRANKLY, ANDREA...

Andrea McArdle, playing Judy Garland in the 1978 TV movie *Rainbow*, sings "Dear Mr. Gable" to the tune of "You Made Me Love You," serenading a photo of Clark Gable as Rhett Butler. However, the scene is based on a real-life incident that happened a year before the filming of *Gone With the Wind* (1939).

USA YESTERDAY

Although the Al Pacino *Scarface* (1983) is set in 1980, there is a shot in which a *USA Today* vending machine can be seen; the paper didn't begin publishing until 1982. In another scene, there's a shot of a billboard advertising a 1984 Corvette.

THEY MIGHT BE GETTING A LITTLE RIPE BY NOW

Sharp-eyed Bart Andrews reports that there are more than a few continuity errors in the 1989 *Steel Magnolias*—among the more interesting of which is that Sally Fields' two teenage sons remain the same age throughout the picture, even though about three years transpire. They don't change hairstyles or clothes.

HELLO...HOW'S THAT AGAIN?

Dolly Levi does her matchmaking work at the turn of the century in Barbra Streisand's 1969 *Hello, Dolly!* Some of Hollywood's most elaborate sets were built for the production—many of which still remain at the entrance to the 20th Century-Fox lot in West Los Angeles. But when *Dolly* was filmed and the sets were dressed, a wrecked but relatively modern automobile was left sitting by the railroad track.

THE DRUMMER STUMBLES

As if *The Cotton Club* (1984) wasn't plagued with enough problems, a musician noticed that the drum heads used in the movie are of modern synthetic materials—not the type used by drummers in the 1930s, the time in which the movie was set, when drum heads were natural skins. And while we're vamping, we should point out that Fred Astaire plays the drums in one scene with wire whisks in *Daddy Long Legs* (1955). In the next shot, he's using wooden drum sticks.

NOW YOU SEE IT, NOW YOU DON'T

Perhaps the peskiest of continuity errors are the instances where something appears in one scene, then disappears in another—often reappearing in yet another.

Again, one of the problems can be the non-sequential manner in which movies are shot. For example, all of an actor's close-ups will be filmed, then the camera moved and refocused, the sets relighted, then the "long shots" will be filmed. If something has gone awry between one setup and another (during which a day or more can transpire)—even though the two will be intercut into a whole when the film is finally edited and assembled—little things can come and go.

Perhaps that's what happened when Yul Brynner was filming his wonderful "Is a Puzzlement" number in *The King and I* (1956). Notice in several of the long shots, he's wearing an earring—one large enough to dangle and flicker. But, in the close-ups (including an extreme close-up that goes right to his ear), there's no earring. (Several times throughout the song, the earring can be seen to come and go, and even change ears.)

NUMBERS, PLEASE

Director Lloyd Bacon mixed actual game footage with his own scenes to create the football sequences in *Knute Rockne—All American* (1940). A very effective approach—except in the game footage the players had uniform numbers, and in the close-ups they didn't.

BUT OFFICER, YOU MUST BE MISTAKEN!

A motorcycle policeman stops Lily Tomlin in *9 to 5* (1980) because she is driving a car with one taillight out and the other blinking. But when she drives away, both lights are working just fine.

EARL SCHEIB IS THERE WHEN YOU NEED HIM

Farrah Fawcett drives a badly-dented Datsun as she is chased through the streets of Acapulco in the 1979 *Sunburn*. The chase leads right into a *corrida*. The Datsun disappears into a tunnel, and emerges into the bull-ring with nary a scratch or dent. Also, in the lobby card for this comedy, it's easy to see the cameraman sitting in the front seat next to Farrah.

CHOPPER REPAIR

In the 1967 James Bond thriller, *You Only Live Twice*, technicians can be seen removing a landing strut from a helicopter. But in later close-ups, the strut is still in place.

81

THE DOORWAY TO WEIGHT LOSS

Walter Matthau had a heart attack during the filming of *The Fortune Cookie* (1966). It was five months later before he came back to finish the scene that was being shot earlier, so this time he came through the door forty pounds lighter!

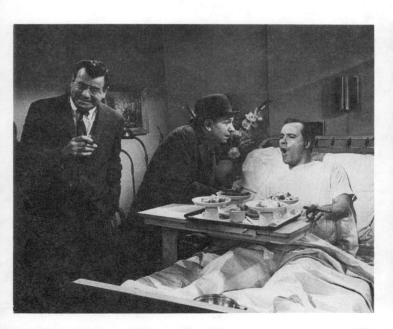 

MEET THE CREW

When the set is full of people, there's a chance that a crew member will accidentally slip into a scene, remaining there for time and all eternity—as does the crew member in the Clark Gable/Marion Davies movie *Cain and Mabel* (1936) who wanders onto the screen, then exits sheepishly.

FINGERING THE KILLER

The jewelry gremlins did a bit of sabotage to Alfred Hitchcock's 1936 spy thriller *Sabotage*. During a scene in which Sylvia Sidney plots to kill Oscar Homolka with a carving knife, you can see a ring on the third finger of her left hand. A few frames later, the ring is gone.

MISSING CHILDREN

When Thomas Mitchell makes his speech in church in *High Noon* (1952), there are children sitting in the pews along with the adults. Then the children mysteriously disappear, but they're back in the next shot. Thank the Lord.

A TALL ORDER

Super-sized Kevin Peter Hall as the clumsy Bigfoot monster crashes his head through the Hendersons' ceiling in the 1987 *Harry and the Hendersons*. But in the next scene, the ceiling is in perfect condition.

A DELI-CATE MATTER

There are just all sorts of problems with Goldie Hawn's sandwich in *Foul Play* (1978). As she lunches on a park bench, the sandwich is whole, then half-eaten, then uneaten again, then half-eaten, then it has just one bite out of it, then it disappears completely.

A MOMENT OF FREEDOM

When Nick Nolte springs Eddie Murphy out of jail in *48 HRS.* (1982), Murphy is handcuffed. Soon we see Murphy with one arm stretched over the seat back. Then he's handcuffed again.

ANIMATED ANNOYANCES

Assembling an animated film requires meticulous craftsmanship and planning. After all, twenty-four individual drawings ("cels") have to be hand-crafted for each second of the film. We're talking 1,440 drawings per minute.

Nonetheless, errors can creep in. In *Snow White*, there is supposedly a moment where missing cels cause a flicker. And recently, animation buff William Simpson discovered that in the masterful *The Little Mermaid* (1989), Ursula's lipstick tube vanishes from her hand the moment before she applies it; a thimble that Sebastian the Crab catches on his foot disappears, then reappears, then vanishes again; lemon slices disappear from Grimsby's dinner plate; and there are several instances of positioning errors in transitions from long shots to close-ups.

THE BACKGROUND MOVES FORWARD

Just about the most fun a big-league gaffe-spotter can have is finding something totally out of character which mysteriously appears in the background of a scene. The slip can range from equipment actually getting into the shot (microphone booms are major offenders) to some which have become classic goofs.

Airplane vapor trails in the sky bedevil many a period film—especially the wide-open-spaces Westerns. Look for the telltale trails in the 19th century hoss operas like *The Yellow Mountain* (Lex Barker/Mala Powers—1954) and Ray Milland's *A Man Alone* (1955). And in the 1939 *Stagecoach*, even the great John Ford failed to catch the automobile tire tracks that slipped into a shot of his film which was, of course, set back when stagecoaches didn't run on Goodyears.

Directors admit that one of the worst things that can happen is spotting something out of the ordinary in the background of a shot when they're checking over the dailies. At best, they can go back the next day and re-shoot the scene. At worst, they can't afford an expensive refilming to cover up their goof and just have to live with it, hoping that no one will notice. But someone always will. Count on it.

CIRCLE THE WINNEBAGOS

John Wayne was a busy man being both star and director of *The Alamo* (1960). So can we blame him if he didn't notice that mobile trailers appear in the background of several battle scenes…or that we can see a falling stunt man land on a mattress?

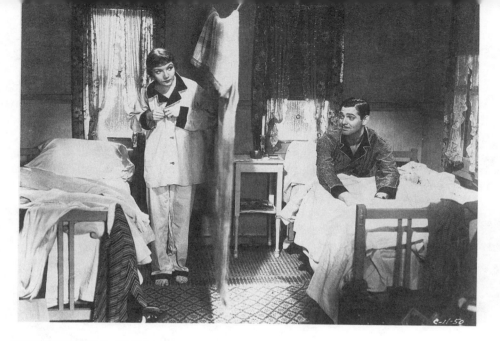

TIME STANDS STILL

In *It Happened One Night* (1934), Clark Gable leaves Claudette Colbert in a tourist cabin. The clock on the wall indicates that it's 2:30 in the morning. He drives to New York, writes a story for the newspaper, and drives back. When he later returns to the room, the clock still reads 2:30. (Of course, he could have been gone *exactly* 24 hours!)

SHOOTING GALLERY

Classic scenes in classic films aren't immune to little background flubs. In Hitchcock's *North by Northwest* (1959), there's a wonderful bit early on in the restaurant scene. A small boy is seated with his family at a table in the background. *Before* Eva Marie Saint reaches into her purse to pull out a gun and shoot Cary Grant, the prescient little boy grimaces and puts his finger in his ears to avoid the noise. (Undoubtedly he remembered from rehearsals that there's a big bang coming.)

IT RAINETH ON BOTH THE RIGHTEOUS AND...

Even though directors try to foster the myth of their omnipotence, they can't count on a rainstorm when they need it. So they have to create it, with upward-pointing spray fixtures. But in *Shoot the Moon* (1982), the rain pattern wasn't set just right. The rain falls only on the actors, while the background remains dry.

IT RAINETH II

In David Lean's classic, *Brief Encounter* (1945), marvelous British actress Celia Johnson runs through a rainstorm, but does a really effective job of dodging the drops. She doesn't get wet!

MAKE MINE DRY, PLEASE

Chevy Chase jumps fully clothed into a lake in *Funny Farm* (1988), then wades out and gets into his car. In the next scene, his clothes are miraculously dry. Dry too are Michael Caine's, when, after swimming to damsel-in-distress Lorraine Gary's rescue in *Jaws the Revenge* (1987), he climbs into her boat without a drop of water on him and with his shirt still neatly pressed.

COME FLY WITH ME

In the 1956 film *Carousel*, set in 1870, a World War II airplane flies across the Booth Bay Harbor. Probably flying Frank Sinatra out—or replacement Gordon MacRae in.

JUST TRUCKING ALONG

As James Garner as the Old West's Bret Maverick is chatting with a railroad station clerk in TV's *The New Maverick* (1978), a white truck crosses the screen from left to right.

JUST TRUCKING ALONG II (The Sequel)

It's the 14th century, and in *Decameron Nights* (1953), Louis Jourdan, playing the pirate Paganino, stands on the deck of his ship preparing to swashbuckle. In the distance, a large white truck drives down a hill.

JUST TRUCKING ALONG III—EXXON IS EVERYWHERE

Modern transportation bedevils the 1979 Peter Sellers version of *The Prisoner of Zenda*. As Sellers and his entourage approach the city in a carriage during a Graustarkian chase scene, a tank truck and two Volkswagens cross the horizon.

TRAFFIC MANAGEMENT

An assistant director can be seen in a jeep waving the extras on in the 1956 *War and Peace*. Wrong war!

ANY OLD PORT IN A STORM

The Maltese Falcon (1941) is set in San Francisco...but, like most movies, was filmed largely in Los Angeles. Thus, when the La Paloma burns, a sign reading "Port of Los Angeles" is seen over a door leading onto a wharf.

MAJOR LEAGUE MISCUES

Although its baseball sequences were set in Cleveland, Ohio, much of the 1989 *Major League* was filmed in Milwaukee, Wisconsin. Thus, even though the game is supposedly being played in Cleveland's stadium, we see the logo of Milwaukee station WTMJ over the scoreboard—which also features a Milwaukee Brewers logo.

And as if that wasn't enough, there are problems with the scoreboard clock—the same kind of gaffe that hearkens back to 1934 when time apparently stood still in the aforementioned *It Happened One Night.* In *Major League,* the clock reads 10:40 (presumably A.M., since the scene is played in sunlight—but then how many major league games are played in the morning?). However after a base hit, a conference on the mound, and a scene in the broadcast booth, there's a cut back to the clock—which still reads 10:40.

Later in the movie, the clock remains at 10:20 (P.M., we suppose, since it's dark outside) from the seventh inning on during a playoff game.

SON OF FILM FLUBS

While taking a train trip in *Son of Frankenstein* (1938), Basil Rathbone calls attention to the weirdly stunted trees. One of the trees manages to pass by the train window three times. Incidentally, this was Boris Karloff's last film as the Frankenstein monster. Was he felled by the trees?

GROUNDS FOR BURIAL

In Stephen King's *Pet Sematary* (1989), Dale Midkiff, playing Dr. Louis Creed, sits next to his son's grave. A bouquet of purple flowers adorns the one to his right. After a cutaway to a recurring zombie apparition, the camera returns to Creed, and the purple flowers are now yellow. Also, the once-hazy sky has miraculously and instantly cleared.

GEORGIA ON YOUR MIND

Next time you revel in *Gone With the Wind,* scan the scene at the famous Battle of Atlanta panorama. See if you can tell which of the wounded laid out at the railway station are live actors, and which are dummies. You might as well know, too, that as Scarlett runs through the streets from Atlanta, she passes an electric light. Isn't it interesting that progressive Atlanta had electric lights in the Civil War era, while all those other cities were having to use gas light? Frankly, Scarlett ...

PROP PROBLEMS

Props—from the vases, statues, flowers and other things that dress a set to the objects that characters carry in their hands, can be an unending source of continuity problems. When a set is shut down for the day, it's generally festooned with "hot set" signs, to warn anyone who ambles through not to touch anything. When one shot is spliced to another in the editing room, a prop that has been moved will "jump" from one place to another, causing a real distraction.

But even the simplest of scenes, such as the act of having a character enter an elevator on one floor and emerge on another, take hours and hours of changing camera setups, re-lighting, and rehearsing the actors to make sure that everything about the scene looks natural.

Even the entering of a room can be time-consuming and complex. The actor approaches the door, puts his hand on the knob, and opens it in one shot. Then everything is moved to the other side of the door, lights are reset, the actors repositioned, and then we see the actor from the front, opening the door again and coming through it into the room. That mere act alone can take up a morning's work, and allow for glitches and gremlins to creep into a film. Case histories:

DOGGING TEA AND SYMPATHY

A pair of china dogs are back to back in a master shot (overall wide view) of a scene in Vincente Minnelli's *Tea and Sympathy* (1956). But when the camera moves in for close-ups, the dogs are face to face.

O.K. YOU COUNT IT!

In *The Thomas Crown Affair* (1968), the haul from the first bank robbery totals $2,660,527.62, as explained by the police. It is broken down into 16,240 $20 bills, 19,871 $10 bills, 34,645 $5 bills, and 129,000 $1 bills, adding up to only $825,735, as later detailed by a secretary. That, of course, makes the whole greater than the sum of its parts.

THE FIFTH WHEEL (AND THE SIXTH)

It's one of filmdom's most memorable chase scenes—Steve McQueen's race up and down the hills of San Francisco in *Bullitt* (1968). Notice that during the course of the chase, the Dodge Charger which McQueen pursues loses three hubcaps. but when it crashes into a wall at the chase's end, three (more) hubcaps fly through the air.

Of course, such chases have to be carefully choreographed in order to look realistic. Even though they're usually shot on empty streets very early in the morning, extras drive other cars through the scenes to add verisimilitude. But notice how the same little Volkswagen bug keeps coming into the *Bullitt* chase scene time after time. Speedy little dude, isn't it?

BOUNCING BOULDERS

If you've ever been on a movie studio tour, you've seen the foam-rubber boulders that are often used to prevent damage to actors in landslide scenes and the like. The fake boulders can look very real—unless they bounce. In *Raiders of the Lost Ark* (1981), watch as Harrison Ford shoves a boulder out of the escape hatchway. Then watch as the shadow of the boulder bounces.

... WOBBLING WALLS

And in a similar vein, in *The Jewel of the Nile* (1985), Michael Douglas does a Tarzan rope-swing into a rock wall, which "gives" as he hits it.

...AND POTTY CROWNS

In *The Wizard of Oz* (1939), the cowardly lion's "crown," made from a broken flower pot, bounces when it falls from his head at the end of "If I Were King of the Forest."

JUST A LITTLE (FALSE) NOTE

Songbird Jeanette MacDonald pens a note in Victor Herbert's period musical *Naughty Marietta* (1935). But she writes it with a modern fountain pen.

THOSE MAGNIFICENT YET-TO-BE-BUILT AUTOMOBILES

The car that Steve Railsback drives in *The Stunt Man* (1980) is identified in dialogue as a Duesenberg, one of the most luxurious cars ever made. The car crashes through a bridge railing and into the river in a scene set in 1917. However, the first Duesenberg wasn't built until 1920.

A ROLE TO DIE FOR

Paul Boller and Ronald L. Davis report in their delightful *Hollywood Anecdotes* an incident during the filming in 1934 of *The Thin Man*. A bevy of Metro character actors are seated around a refectory table for a long tracking shot by director W.S. "Woody" Van Dyke. A bespectacled veteran actor with a black mustache, at the head of the table, is delivering a long speech, as the camera trucks along, getting the reactions of each character. As the camera got to the end, the actor concluded, "And that's all I have to say," at which point he sat down and actually died. But Van Dyke reportedly wouldn't allow the body to be taken from the set until he had knelt behind the dead actor with his viewfinder and set up an over-the-shoulder shot. "All right, take him out, but leave the coat," he barked. Which garment he then put on another actor to finish the scene with over-the-shoulder shots.

ROSES ARE RED, CARNATIONS AREN'T

Business executive Katharine Hepburn leaves her high-rise office in the 1957 comedy *Desk Set*, carrying a bouquet of white carnations. Wonder what happened in the elevator on the way down? When she emerges into the building's lobby, the flowers have become pink.

A SACK FULL OF TROUBLE

Bill Murray decides to go AWOL in *Stripes* (1981), but buddy Harold Ramis catches up with him and wrestles him to the ground. From one camera angle, Murray's head rests on his duffle bag; from another, the bag is at his feet.

AW, STUFF IT

The makers of *Terror in the Jungle* (1968) used stuffed animals to simulate the real thing in several scenes—but weren't consistent. A stuffed lion in one scene becomes a stuffed tiger in another, and the stuffed tiger becomes a real tiger.

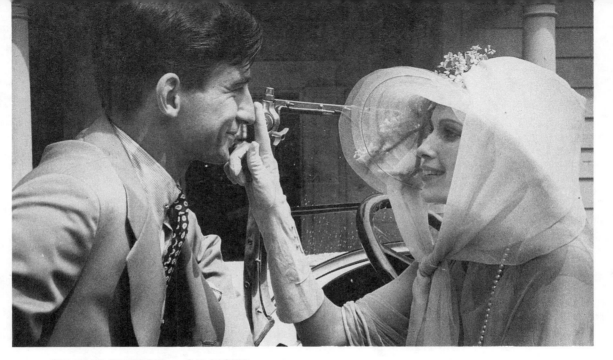

OF THE PERIOD...OR NOT?

The Great Gatsby (1974) is a lush period piece...and antique cars add much to the film's authenticity—except when a 1934 Packard cruises by in a scene set in 1925. Robert Young, Jr., spotted the error, and he should know. The Packard was his own car, a custom-crafted Super Eight Dual-Cowl Sports Sedan.

JOKER-ING ASIDE

The label on the bottle the Joker is hawking in the 1989 *Batman* is a dead giveaway that the movie was British-made note the spelling of "moisturizing" with the English—"s."

BIRDY, DO YOU HAVE THE *TIMES*?

Even the master of deductive reasoning can slip up occasionally. In Billy Wilder's *The Private Life of Sherlock Holmes* (1970), Robert Stephens says that a newspaper in the bottom of a bird cage is "The Inverness Courier," but when the camera moves in for a closer look, it's "The Inverness Times."

AN INTERNATIONAL METROPOLIS

Superman's Metropolis was actually in England during the filming of *Superman IV: Quest for Peace* (1987). Perhaps that's why the *Daily Planet* is identified as "Your Favourite Newspaper" (the British spelling of "favorite"). Also, while we are to assume that the subway chase scene takes place in New York, it's easy to see that it was shot in the London Underground, with its round tunnels, straphangers, and uniquely-shaped cars.

IT MIGHT GIVE YOU A HANGOVER, TOO

The film is about a mad composer—and someone went just a little mad in assembling the props for *Hangover Square* (1945). Although the introductory titles set the date of the action at 1899, a theatre program in one scene is clearly dated 1903.

DOESN'T EVERYTHING?

A newspaper used as a prop in *Triple Cross* (1967), the World War II Yul Brynner spy yarn, has a story about the price of the Concorde going up again. Since jets weren't around during that war, let alone the SST, one can only wonder why the French were thinking about going supersonic!

YOU'VE SEEN ONE, YOU'VE SEEN THEM ALL

During the course of *Triple Cross*, the German luxury liner *Lusitania* is sunk. The ship pictured on the front of a newspaper reporting the event has two stacks. The *Lusitania* had four.

SORRY, WRONG NUMBER

Mama Rose, in the person of Rosalind Russell, receives a telegram in *Gypsy* (1962). But the number on the address on it isn't the same as the one on her door, so how did that Western Union guy find her?

ALL THE NEWS THAT FITS

Take a close look at the newspaper that Sheila McCarthy holds as she reads a review to Paule Baillargeon in *I've Heard the Mermaids Singing* (1987). The newspaper is the "Toronto Globe & Star," and when she folds it down you see an ad for New York's Radio City Music Hall "Christmas Spectacular." And the "Arts and Leisure" section on the back looks suspiciously like the one in *The New York Times*. That's because there is no "Toronto Globe & Star"—it's a mock-up paper which the prop people obviously created out of Section 2 of the *Sunday New York Times*.

BOOGIE WOOGIE BOO-BOO

Sean Penn puts a record of The Andrews Sisters singing "Boogie Woogie Bugle Boy" on the turntable during *Racing With the Moon* (1984). Even though there was careful attention to 1940s detail during the movie, the record he uses has a Columbia label—but Patty, Maxene and LaVerne recorded for Decca. (Sean, of course, could have been using a compilation version marketed by Columbia Special Products.)

SHOT TO SHOT

The process of making a movie is not linear. A scene may be shot early in the day, and the one that appears but a second afterwards may be filmed later that same evening, the next day, or perhaps even weeks later.

Once again, it's the job of the script supervisor to make certain (hopefully) that there is an exact match from one shot to the next, no matter how much time has elapsed in between. But things happen...things get overlooked. And even the most minute slips get caught—and show up in books like this one!

In *Cocktail* (1988), when Tom Cruise and Lisa Banes pass the Regency Theatre in Manhattan on the way to an art show next door, the marquee sports a fancy cover for *Barfly* (inside joke?). They go in, he picks a fight, and less than three minutes later, he's out on the street, doubling over in agony, because the feature has changed to *Casablanca*.

THE NOM-DE-STEAM VANISHES

In the 1938 version of *The Lady Vanishes*, dear old Dame May Whitty's Miss Froy writes her name on the steam-frosted train window. But a few shots later, the writing has moved to another place, and is entirely different. And, just to continue in the great tradition of continuity errors stretching across the years, in Cybill Shepherd's 1979 remake of the same film, her dress shoes magically become her trademark running shoes as she chases the train.

THE DEVIL MADE ME DO IT

In *National Lampoon's Animal House* (1978), the word "Satan," which is written on a blackboard, looks totally different from one shot to another.

A BLOODY LITTLE GAFFE

Just before young Indy (River Phoenix) receives his trademark fedora (in 1989's *Indiana Jones and the Last Crusade*), he gets roughed up and the dribbling blood on his chin switches from the left side to the right.

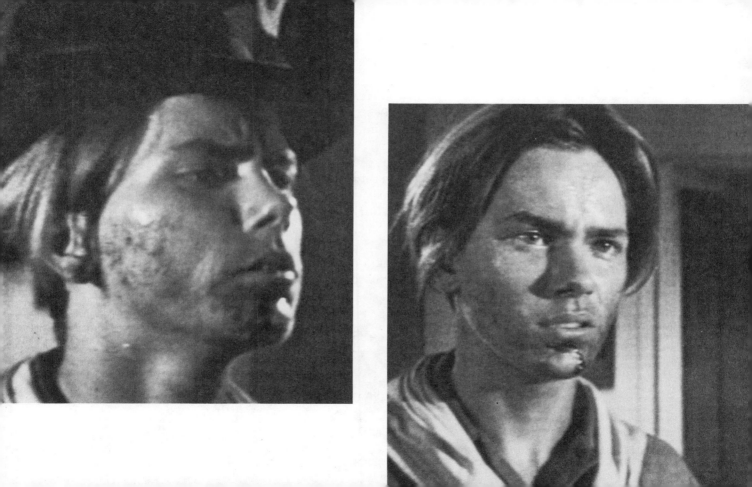

NOBODY NOTICED

Filmdom's trickiest continuity gaffes are the little things that no one seemed to notice at the time—ones spotted by only the most eagle-eyed moviegoer. Usually, they're the things of today that just don't make sense in the films of yesteryear.

As an example, look closely at the cavewomen in the 1966 *One Million Years B.C.* with Raquel Welch. Isn't it interesting that even back then they were able to buy false eyelashes? Apparently, you have to look your best to get a caveman to bash you over your head and drag you by the hair into his lair.

BACHELOR PARTY

Billy Wilder's *Double Indemnity* (1944) is one of filmdom's great classics—but it also contains a classic example of the little things that seem to slip by. Even though Fred MacMurray has been established as a carefree, never-married bachelor, throughout the entire film he wears a wide gold wedding band.

IN THIS VALE OF TEARS

Vicki Vale's name is spelled "Vicky Vale" on the cover of a magazine featuring her photographs in the 1989 *Batman*. And in another Jack Nicholson flick, during the course of *The Shining* (1980), the first name of the previous caretaker changes.

HOLY BAT GAFFE

When Jack Nicholson as the Joker and his evil band are vandalizing paintings in *Batman* (1989), one villian puts pink handprints all over a portrait. In the next shot, the handprints have disappeared.

GONNA MAKE MY BROWN EYES BLUE

In a flashback in the 1989 *Batman*, the young Jack Nicholson has blue eyes. The later Jack Nicholson has brown eyes!

MIRACULOUS DISAPPEARANCE

And in the same *Batman*, police lieutenant Eckhardt appears at the gate outside the Axis Chemical Company with a stubble of beard. Moments later, he's inside the plant—clean shaven.

THE NAKED TRUTH

One of the best slips of movie logic takes place when Claude Rains, in the elusive title role of *The Invisible Man* (1933), uses his invisibility to elude the police near the end of the film. He strips completely naked, head to toe. But take a look at the footprints in the snow that the police follow as they track him. They're made by feet wearing shoes!

BRIDGING THE GAP

Dustin Hoffman should be glad he wasn't on San Francisco's Bay Bridge during the 1989 earthquake—the one that split the span between San Francisco and Berkeley. In *The Graduate* (1967), he was supposedly driving to Berkeley. But in the shots where he's on the bridge, he's heading toward San Francisco.

TRANSCENDENT AND TRANSLUCENT

The special effects which blend flying birds with human actors in Alfred Hitchcock's *The Birds* (1963) are remarkable...so remarkable, in fact, that when assembling the special effects for a sequence set on a sunny day in one scene, no one noticed that the creatures that chase the children cast no shadows!

GEE WIZ!

Think about it. When the Scarecrow gets his diploma in *The Wizard of Oz* (1939), he shows off his new-found brainpower with the statement: "The sum of the square roots of any two sides of an isosceles triangle is equal to the square root of the remaining side." Ahem. Wrong. So much for the scarecrow's intellect. David Fradkin points out in *Los Angeles* magazine that in Pythagorean theorem, the square of the length of the hypotenuse (longest side) of a *right* triangle is equal to the sum of the *squares* of the lengths of the other two sides.

JUST A LITTLE...OUT OF STEP

One of the goose-stepping Munchkins is very much out of (goose) step in *The Wizard of Oz* (1939).

REFLECT ON THIS

Risking the wrath of the Trekkies (or, as they prefer to be called, the Trekkers), it must be pointed out that in *Star Trek—The Motion Picture* (1979), when the *Starship Enterprise* flies past Jupiter and its moons, the light comes in at such an angle that there's a half moon, a crescent, and a full moon. Moons are, after all, reflective bodies and the implication is that the light comes from several different sources in differing directions.

FEATS OF EXTREME GRAVITY

Well, let's face it. Stanley Kubrick couldn't shoot *2001—A Space Odyssey* (1968) in a weightless environment, so he just had to make do with special effects to get all the floating objects and people to look right in his meticulously-crafted masterpiece. However, even this classic is not without its oversights. Look for the time when Floyd sucks some liquid food from a container—and the remainder of the liquid drops back to the bottom, just as it would in earth's gravity. There's also a scene at the Orbiter Hilton where it appears that William Sylvester is blowing the food down the straw rather than sucking it up.

And at another point in the movie, the captain leans on the back of Floyd's chair. No mean feat in an environment where gravity isn't pulling on your own feet. Also—when an astronaut leaves the pod in a free-float to work on the AE35 unit, you can see the shadow of the cables attached to his feet.

ON THE OTHER HAND

Even though we have no desire to get into "Indy-bashing" (see an earlier-mentioned *Raiders of the Lost Ark* gaffe), for the sake of historical veracity, it should be pointed out that in *Indiana Jones and the Last Crusade* (1989), when Our Hero asks Hitler for an autograph, Der Führer signs his name with "ph"—as in *Adolph*, rather than the correct Germanic *Adolf*. And, just to compound the crime, the actor playing Hitler signs the autograph with his right hand. Der Führer was a southpaw.

WELL, MAYBE HE CONVERTED

In previous *Rocky* films, it had been pretty well established that Burgess Meredith's character was Irish. But in *Rocky III* (1982), Sylvester Stallone, as the muscular big guy, donned a yarmulke and mourned as his mentor was given a Jewish funeral.

A BURNING QUESTION

Did anyone notice that as Ginger Rogers teases Fred Astaire with "A Fine Romance" in *Swing Time* (1936), he takes a few puffs on his pipe then puts it—lit—in his jacket pocket? David Hajdu did, and wonders how Fred stayed so cool during the rest of the number.

LICENSE TO KILL

John Carpenter's horror classic *Halloween* (1978) is set in a town in Illinois. How many noticed that the cars have California license plates?

THE SIX...ER, SEVEN, SHOOTER

Donald Pleasence as "Loomis" fires six shots at the Michael Myers creature in the 1978 *Halloween*. But when the moment is recalled in a flashback in the sequel, *Halloween II* (1981), Pleasence fires seven shots in the exact same scene.

FOOTPRINTS IN THE SNOWS OF TIME

When Ronald Colman gets lost in a blizzard in the mountains of Tibet in Frank Capra's 1937 classic *Lost Horizon*, he rolls down a mountain on which "no man" has ever set foot. But, if that's true, what's the explanation for a long set of footprints in the snow in the foreground of the shot?

SPOOKY DOINGS

In *Poltergeist* (1982), as writer David Hajdu notes, director Tobe Hooper had the actors walk up the steps backwards to create a supernatural effect, then reverse the film to obtain his spooky objective.

And he gleefully defuses the spectacular, glitzy effect when Esther Williams rises from the water with fiery sparklers in her headdress in *Neptune's Daughter* (1949). Run the tape backwards and you'll see that she was actually *lowered* into the water to create the effect, with the sparklers being snuffed as she went in.

SHINING MOMENTS

They may be trapped in a blinding, devastating snowstorm in *The Shining* (1980), but Jack Nicholson and family are watching Warner Bros' film *The Class of '44*, and the reception is perfect. Maybe they had a VCR hidden away somewhere at a time when few homes, much less a vacation lodge, had video players.

NO FLOSSING ON KRYPTON

The subject: Christopher Reeve's portrayal of *Superman* (1978). Our hero may well be invincible—able to leap tall buildings in a single bound and to fend off bullets with his "S" -embossed chest—but obviously, he was no match for the dentist. The Man of Steel has fillings in his teeth.

AT THE DROP OF A HAT

A super-sensitive floor is a key plot device in *Treasure of the Four Crowns* (1983). But when a hat is dropped on it, no one noticed that the alarm didn't go off!

MIRROR IMAGES

Mirrors—or anything else that's reflective and shiny—can be among the most troublesome props on a set, close behind food, drink and cigarettes. Camera crews have to be extremely careful that they aren't seen in reflections from anything that's shiny. And mirrors aren't the only problem. Storefronts, with their wide expanses of glass, are a particular problem.

Take *Carmen Jones* (1954), for instance. The camera tracks along as Dorothy Dandridge strolls down a shop-filled street. The camera crew can be seen reflected in the store windows.

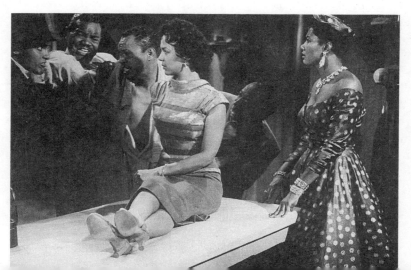

Similarly, in *A Christmas Carol* (1951), the camera crew can be seen in the mirror behind Alistair Sim in Dickensian London. And in the Meryl Streep/Robert De Niro *Falling in Love* (1984), you can see the reflection of the camera in a scene involving a mirror.

Then there are some other mirror problems on which you might wish to reflect:

MONSTROUS IMAGES

It's a basic tenet of vampire lore that the undead creatures don't cast reflections, right? Well, in the 1979 *Dracula*, when Dr. Von Helsing goes in search of a female vampire in an underground cavern, his first glimpse of her is a reflection in a pool of water. Hmmmm…

MONSTROUS IMAGES II (The Sequel)

When *Abbott and Costello Meet Frankenstein* in their 1948 movie, Dracula makes his appearance to lust, as usual, after the blood of healthy young girls. As he is about to attack a comely damsel when she steps back, the vampire is seen in the mirror. Once again, the filmmakers didn't reflect on the legendary vampire lore.

1572-61

MONSTROUS IMAGES III (Son of the Sequel)

The camera crew can be seen reflected in the glass covering Jeff Goldblum's pod in *The Fly* (1988).

And how often have you noticed that in practically every movie ever made that has its actors seated in a car, when a shot is made through the front windshield, there is no rearview mirror? It's generally been removed so as not to obstruct the actors' faces.

BUDDY, HAVE YOU GOT THE TIME?

If there's ever a gremlin that's lurking around just waiting for a moment's inattention by a film costumer, it's the one that is in charge of watches and wedding rings. After all, the roles in historical or period films are being played by modern-day actors for whom wearing anything from Rolexes to Reeboks is such a routine, everyday thing that it's very easy for these items to go unnoticed.

IT'S HALF PAST TEN, M'LADY

Not to be outdone by the Greeks, a time-conscious character in the British-made *The Viking Queen* (1967) is clearly seen wearing a wristwatch.

EXCUSE ME, M'LORD. DO YOU HAVE THE TIME?

In Cecil B. DeMille's 1935 epic, *The Crusades*, the king actually flips back his cape and looks at his watch!

HOLY MOSES

Perhaps the most egregious appearance of a watch in a historical movie happens in one of the greatest epics of them all—*The Ten Commandments* (1956)—when a blind man is seen wearing one on his wrist. Wonder if they made Braille timepieces back then?

THE REVOLT BEGINS AT NINE O'CLOCK SHARP

In *Spartacus* (1960), it seems that some soldiers didn't want to be late for battle. Look closely. You'll see several wearing wristwatches. And some of them wanted to make sure that they'd be sure-footed in the heat of battle. You can see more than one soldier charging up a hill wearing tennis shoes.

SEASONAL SLIPUPS

'Tis the season…or 'tisn't it? Seems like "seasonal" blunders can appear from time to time in your favorite films, and usually there's an easy explanation. The season in which the film is shot is often far away from the one in which it is set.

Thus we're able to see the actor's breath in *In the Heat of the Night* (1967), even though the film is set in the hot, sultry Deep South.

THIS IS JULY?

In *Jaws* (1975), even though a picnic scene is set on the Fourth of July, the trees are winter-bare. (The scene was shot in May, before spring had completely sprung on Martha's Vineyard.)

A newscaster comments that it is "a nice spring day" in *The Day the Earth Stood Still* (1951). However, later in the film, it's revealed that the action takes place in July.

LAWN CARE

On the other hand, in the 1989 TV movie, *Cross of Fire*, the leading lady is encountered dutifully raking leaves on her front lawn, while all the trees are lush with green foliage—since filming was done in Kansas in mid-July.

TECHNICAL TROUBLES

No matter how professional the crews and attentive the craftmen, niggling technical bloopers slip into film frames. The most common offender is the microphone, since the boom man's primary job is to hold it just outside the camera's view in order to get the best possible sound. But because it's either being hand-held on a long pole or tracked in from overhead, it time and again gets into the frame.

As it did in *Gardens of Stone* (1987), where, in an early scene, the mike is mixed in with some tree branches...right in front of the face of one of the soldiers.

MIKE'S STILL PESKY

Not even comedian John Candy's bulk nor comely Daryl Hannah's charms can detract from the obvious mike that's intruding on more than one scene in *Splash* (1984) ... and there's even one following Dennis Quaid around in a scene in *Suspect* (1987) where he has a lengthy discourse with an older woman.

DAY FOR NIGHT

Movie sound man John Travolta wrecks his car while rushing to save
Nancy Allen in Brian De Palma's *Blow Out* (1981). It's broad daylight when
he is pulled from the wreckage and put in an ambulance. But just seconds
later, he hears Allen screaming through his earphone. He jumps out of
the ambulance to save her—and day has turned to night.

SHADOWING THE STARS

As Scarlett and Melanie minister to the wounded in a sequence in *Gone With the Wind*, the shadows of the two dedicated ladies don't match their movements.

In *Miracle on 34th Street* (1947), on the other hand, a camera shadow follows Edmund Gwenn and John Payne as they walk across a square.

THE SOUND OF SOUND

Sound gaffes are not the easiest things to find in a film. So often, dialogue and sound effects obliterate the goof—but now and again, they are over-looked and remain in the final cut.

Bloopmeister Kermit Schaeffer delighted in pointing out one in the distinguished Raymond Massey's *Abe Lincoln in Illinois* (1940) when, as the train pulls out of the station carrying Lincoln to Washington for his first term as President, the crowd is calling out "Goodbye, Mr. Lincoln." But in the middle of the goodbyes, one of those seeing Abe off clearly can be heard saying "Goodbye, Mr. Massey."

Similarly, in *Star Wars* (1977), near the end of the film when Carrie Fisher as Princess Leia rushes to welcome Luke Skywalker (Mark Hamill) back from the final battle, you hear him shout "Carrie!" It's a bit tough to discern from the noisy tumult, but it's there.

HI, JUDY, JUDY, JUDY

There's considerable debate about what might be a vocal gaffe in the famous "Trolley Song" in *Meet Me in St. Louis* (1944). During one of the verses, it appears that someone, thinking it was just a rehearsal, stopped by the set and said "Hi, Judy!"—and the greeting slipped by and went onto the final track. Liza Minnelli owned up to the story during a PBS tribute to her father, director Vincente Minnelli. But some folks say that it's "Hi ya, Johnny," rhythmically placed to greet John Truett (Tom Drake), the boy next door. Listen, and decide for yourself.

MEANWHILE, BACK IN THE JUNGLE

Remember that familiar, atmospheric "brrr-hoo-hoo-ha-ha" you hear as an establishing sound in just about every jungle movie you've ever seen, no matter if the setting is in Africa, South America, Asia, or a tropical island? Well, it's a ringer—the cry is that of the Australian Kookaburra, a kingfisher that lives only in the Outback and nowhere else on earth, except perhaps in a zoo or in a sound editor's bag of tricks.

CREDIT CHECKS

Film credits are pretty important to the Hollywood community. Days—even weeks—are spent in negotiations to determine just what kind of credit an actor, writer, director or producer gets in a film.

Negotiations can revolve around the size of the type used for the credit in relationship to the title and to fellow artists, the sequence in which it runs, who comes first and who comes last (either of which can be fairly important positions in the credit crawl), whether the name appears singly or with other credits, who gets billed on the left—the preferred location—in the case of two stars of equal importance (at least to their respective agents and managers), and the time it remains on the screen. There have even been instances where an actor walked off a film when he (or she) didn't get the kind of credit thought to be deserved.

A real problem is the spelling of Katharine Hepburn's name. All too often, usually in magazine articles, it's incorrectly spelled Katherine. And it even happened on film. In one of the many fabulous Tracy/Hepburn classics, *State of the Union* (1948), her name is misspelled Katherine Hepburn in the opening crawl.

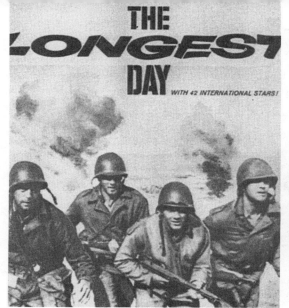 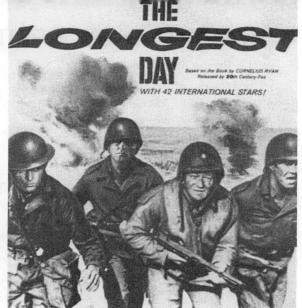

SEND IN THE "A" TEAM

On the ads for the original release of the star-studded *The Longest Day* in 1962, Robert Wagner, Fabian, Paul Anka and Tommy Sands are prominently pictured storming the beach at Normandy, but in the film's 1969 reissue, superimposed atop their uniformed likenesses (to appeal, apparently, to a more mature audience) are the heads of Richard Burton, Robert Mitchum, John Wayne and Henry Fonda.

FU WHO?

One of the leading characters in the 1968 Christopher Lee movie, *The Castle of Fu Manchu*, is referred to as "Ingrid" in the film, "Anna" in the printed synopsis in press handouts, and "Maria" in the end credits.

THE ENEMY WITHIN, THE ENEMY WITHOUT

The credits for *Public Enemy* (1931), that classic film in which James Cagney smashes a grapefruit into Mae Clarke's face, might well have left someone with a little egg on their own face. It turns out that while Louise Brooks is billed as "Bess" in the credits, she didn't appear anywhere in the film. Has anyone checked the famous cutting room floor?

FROM K TO Z

Film and television maven Bart Andrews reports that in the classic *Casablanca* (1942), actor S. Z. "Cuddles" Sakall is identified in the credits as "S. K. Sakall." But Andrews, who reigns as one of the leading experts on television's "I Love Lucy," notes that even that classic show wasn't immune to a credit slip. Although Desi Arnaz was producer and co-star of the series, one season his closing credit read "Dezi."

A BACK OF THE HAND TO CECIL

In both the opening and closing credits of the memorable 1940 horror flick, *The Mummy's Hand*, Cecil Kellaway has to endure the indignity of having his name misspelled twice—as Kelloway. He probably should have slapped the mummy's hand!

LYNCH THE PERSON WHO WROTE THE CREDITS

The credits for the Ku Klux Klan drama *Black Legion* (1936), starring Humphrey Bogart, list Joe Sawyer and Helen Flint playing the roles of Cliff Moore and Pearl Davis. The names of the characters actually were Cliff Summers and Pearl Danvers.

KING LUIS

Just what kind of power does a director have when he can't even get his own named spelled correctly in the credits? The 1935 *Charlie Chan in Egypt* lists director Louis King as "Luis."

A PINT OF GUINNESS, PLEASE

It was one of his greatest roles—Alec Guinness' dedicated, often single-minded Colonel in *Bridge on the River Kwai* (1957). However, the closing crawl for the seven-Oscar blockbuster spells Sir Alec's name as "Guiness," and the gaffe is compounded in many written articles about him. (Liza Minnelli frequently encounters a similar problem—as in the ads for the reissue of *New York, New York* where her last name had only one "n".)

And...while we're at it, you might like to know that since the actual writers who wrote the screenplay for *Bridge on the River Kwai* (Carl Foreman and Michael Wilson) were blacklisted during the nefarious McCarthy Era, the script is credited to novelist Pierre Boulle (who reportedly neither wrote nor spoke English). It was even to Boulle that the Academy of Motion Picture Arts and Sciences gave the Oscar for Best Screenplay—an oversight that was corrected two decades later. However, the credits say that the screenplay is "based on the novel of the same title." Boulle's novel, however, was titled "Bridge *Over* the River Kwai."

A BRIEF GLOSSARY OF TERMS USED IN "FILM FLUBS"

ACTION: The events that happen in front of the camera; third in the classic sequence of "Lights...camera...action!" Also the director's call to start the scene moving.

BEST BOY: The assistant chief electrician (Best Boy/Electric) or the assistant chief grip (Best Boy/Grip). You wondered, now you know.

CAN: Storage for the completed footage; "in the can" means that a scene or entire film has been completed.

CONTINUITY: Progression of the film's action from shot to shot. The continuity director or script supervisor keeps track of the film's continuity.

CREDITS: The list of people who worked on the film and their jobs. Credits are split into "front credits," which list key players, directors and executives at the beginning of the film, and "end credits," which normally cover everyone from the stars and the technicians to the person who brings the doughnuts and coffee to the set (Craft Services, if you didn't already know). The end credits roll across the screen in a credit crawl; the front credits rarely crawl. In the good old movie days, all the credits were right up front on eight or nine cards. This all changed with *Superman* and its twelve-minute end credit crawl of literally hundreds of names.

DAILIES (also called RUSHES): The film footage shot during one day is usually processed and viewed on the next by the key people involved with the production—usually the producer, director, cinematographer, script supervisor and film editor. This gives them the opportunity to look for technical problems, as well as to check performances and line readings by the actors.

DOLLY: The wheeled platform that holds the camera and the camera operator. Due to the way it can move either forward or side-to-side, the dolly is usually called a "crab dolly." The worker who physically moves it around is called the "dolly grip."

ESTABLISHING SHOT: Normally, a wide-angle shot of a room or out-door setting to orient the viewer to the location where the action is taking place, and often to establish a mood. Frequently called a "long shot."

FLASHBACK: A backwards jump in the time of the action, usually used to clarify a plot point or explain a situation—or, in some cases, to pad the film and drag out the action.

FRAME: An individual picture that, when projected at the usual twenty-four frames per second, creates—due to "persistence of vision"—the illusion of movement on the screen. As a verb, "frame" means to compose the image in the camera's viewfinder. In other words, the director or cinematographer "frames" what you will see on the screen.

GAFFER: The chief electrician on a film set (bet you always wondered who that was, didn't you!).

GRIP: A physical laborer on a movie set; similar to a stagehand, but don't tell that to his or her union.

HOT SET: A set that is actively being used for filming, or is ready for use.

LOCATION: A site for shooting that is away from the studio (as in "on location").

MASTER SHOT: Similar to the "establishing shot," the master shot sets up the situations to which other scenes are related—often used first before closeups of the conversations between actors. The master shot generally is filmed first, complete with all dialogue and actions. Individual head shots (one-shots or two-shots) are done separately with the same dialogue and actions, and then spliced in during the editing process to create scene continuity.

MATTE SHOTS: A matte is a specially-designed photographic mask which allows the "sandwiching" of one image into another—usually for special effects. In a matte shot, an actor may well be working on but a tiny portion of a scene; then the film is matted into a larger portion of film—usually a painted background. The matte shot is generally used to create the illusion of great size and depth—or to overlay elaborate special effects devices. A "traveling matte" is a movable mask that allows movement from two different scenes to be integrated into one. In a "Blue Screen" matting process (chroma-key), the actors work in front of a blue background, which is dropped out during final assembly and replaced with a background from another locale.

M.O.S.: Shooting without an accompanying sound track. Legend has it that the term derives from "mit out sound," used by German director Lothar Mendes.

OVER THE SHOULDER: A shot taken from over the shoulder of one actor usually looking toward another. But it can also be used to establish the character's point of view.

PLOT: The main story line of a film; a "plot point" is something that happens during the unfolding of the story to turn the action toward a particular direction.

POINT OF VIEW (POV): In essence, what would be seen through an actor's eyes in his or her point of view. This is duplicated by the camera to give the audience the same point of view.

PRODUCER: Think of the producer as the Chief Executive on a particular film project. The producer usually instigates the film project, hires the writers and supervises script development, arranges for the financing, and generally manages the company that oversees the individual production. There's also an "Executive Producer," who, on quite a number of films, is merely somebody's brother-in-law.

PRODUCTION VALUES: The sum total of generally intangible factors contributing to the quality of a motion picture, or the lack thereof. Production values, as established by the film's budget, range from the quality of the people who work on the set to the costumes, scenery, art direction, and the like.

PROP: Any movable item—other than furniture—that is used on the set and in the scene. "Hand props" are the items that actors actually carry—ranging from guns to bouquets. The props are managed by the Property Master.

PROJECTION PLATE: Usually a slide which is projected onto a background to create a scene. On some sets, screens cover exterior windows and projection plates are used to create the scene that might be seen through the window.

REVERSE: A shot taken from an angle approximately 180 degrees from the preceding one. Normally used in a scene involving a two-actor conversation or entry through a doorway.

SCENE: A division of the film's action—usually, that which takes place at a single location. Can be one shot or a series.

WRAP: As in "wrap-up," when a scene or a film is wrapped, it is completed—thus, the term "it's a wrap" frequently heard on the set...or "are we wrapped?" often asked by actors and technicians ready to head home for the day.

This glossary is a wrap.

ENDNOTE

The real challenge in bringing a book such as this to a close is knowing just when to stop and strike the set. Every time I bring up the subject of the book, someone recalls a favorite flub of which I probably wasn't aware. Or, while I'm in the process of doing some other research, an article turns up listing a few more continuity slipups. So when to stop? Right now! We have to get this thing into print!

Perhaps there should be a bit of an apologia at this point. As a devoted moviegoer and someone who looks upon filmmaking as an art form (well, some of the time!), I should point out that even though this book points out some of the screen's famous errors, it celebrates film as a unique type of entertainment which involves its audience as does perhaps none other. It celebrates the thousands of people who are involved in the making of films, too. I truly hope that no one feels that pointing out a film's little flaws is a denigration of the hours and hours, even years and years, of loving care that go into taking an idea through the many processes that put it on the screen.

Perhaps that's why a sharp-eyed film fan reacts with such glee when a flaw is spotted—the flubs are anomalies, infrequent and so difficult to catch. Of the thousands of films that the industry has created, we've only talked about a couple of hundred. And even the most diligent of movie mavens can recall only a very few goofs, gaffes and flubs from a lifetime of filmgoing.

And I should point out that as hard as we try not to make our own gaffes in a book about gaffes, if we've slipped and flubbed ourselves, we'd like to hear about it—and will be sure to make the correction in future editions.

That being said...if there's one overriding characteristic of the eagle-eyed, perceptive film fault-finders who spot moviedom's funny little blunders, it's the overpowering urge to share them. Keeping a gaffe to one's self is just no fun. You just have to tell someone. So tell us, and we'll pass it on!

When you catch a fumble in a film, let us know about it. Or if you'd like to share some of the lore about any of the slipups mentioned herein, we're all ears! If we can use your contributions in a future edition of FILM FLUBS, they will be gratefully acknowledged. Write:

FILM FLUBS
7510 Sunset Blvd., #100
Hollywood, CA 90046

Let us know about the flubs you spot in television programs, too. Who knows where all this flub-spotting could lead!

Bill Givens
March, 1990

TITLE INDEX

154